The Boxcar Children® Mysteries

THE MYSTERY OF THE STOLEN BOXCAR
created by
GERTRUDE CHANDLER WARNER

Illustrated by Charles Tang

ALBERT WHITMAN & Company
Morton Grove, Illinois

f W arner

Library of Congress Cataloging-in-Publication Data
Warner, Gertrude Chandler, 1890-1979
The mystery of the stolen boxcar/
created by Gertrude Chandler Warner;
illustrated by Charles Tang.
p. cm. — (The Boxcar children mysteries)
Summary: The Alden children plan to ride in their boxcar
at theGreenfield Founders' Day Parade, but the newly
refurbished boxcar is stolen a couple of days before the big event.
ISBN 0-8075-5423-5 (hardcover).
ISBN 0-8075-5424-3 (paperback).
[1. Mystery and detective stories. 2. Parades–Fiction.]
I. Tang, Charles, ill. II. Title. III. Series:
Warner, Gertrude Chandler, 1890-
Boxcar children mysteries.
PZ7.W244 Mxqo 1995   95-30926
[Fic]–dc20   CIP
                                            AC

Cover art by David Cunningham.

482767

Contents

CHAPTER 1

The Newspaper Article

"Henry! Jessie! Violet! Benny!" Mrs. McGregor called across the backyard. She held up a newspaper. Mrs. McGregor was the housekeeper for the Alden family.

Ten-year-old Violet Alden, who'd been playing catch with her six-year-old brother Benny and their dog, Watch, turned around and ran toward Mrs. McGregor.

Their older sister Jessie, who was twelve, and their older brother Henry, who was fourteen, were repairing a bicycle tire nearby.

When they heard Mrs. McGregor, they came quickly over.

"Our picture! Our picture!" said Benny excitedly.

Mrs. McGregor handed the newspaper to Henry. Sure enough, right there on the front page was a photograph of all four of the Alden children, and Watch, too. They were standing in front of their old, red boxcar.

Underneath the photograph were the words, "A part of Greenfield history," and a short article about the Aldens and their boxcar.

The story was one of several articles the newspaper was doing on the history of the town. That was because the anniversary of the founding of Greenfield was coming up.

The town of Greenfield was holding a big Founders' Day celebration. The Aldens were going to have a special Founders' Day dinner to celebrate, too.

"Look, Watch!" said Benny. "You're in the picture! See? Sitting on the stump in front of our boxcar."

Watch wagged his tail.

"Let's take this photograph and put it up in our boxcar," suggested Jessie. "May we have the newspaper, Mrs. McGregor?"

"Grandfather's not home," Violet pointed out. "He hasn't seen it yet."

Mrs. McGregor smiled. "He knew it was going to be in the newspaper today. He's planning to buy extra copies. I'm going to cut the picture out of one of the copies and put it on the refrigerator. And you can keep this one."

"Thank you," said Jessie.

"Don't forget, I need you to go to the grocery store for me a little later," Mrs. McGregor reminded them.

"We won't," promised Henry.

"I'll get some scissors so we can cut the picture and the article out," said Violet.

"And some tape, too," Henry said.

Violet walked back to the house with Mrs. McGregor to get the tape and scissors. The others went out to the boxcar and sat on the edge of the open doorway to admire the picture.

"They even put Watch's name in," Benny

said, smiling. "We're all famous!"

When Violet came back, she carefully cut out the picture and the article and they put it up in a place of honor on the door of the boxcar. Anyone who came into the boxcar could see the photograph right away.

Jessie returned the rest of the newspaper to the house. As she walked back toward the boxcar, she saw a shiny yellow taxicab pull into the driveway by the house.

A thin man with an enormous mustache that curled up at the ends got out of the cab.

"Little girl!" he called. "Little girl, come here. Where is your grandfather?"

Jessie didn't like being called a little girl, but she walked politely over to the thin man.

"Wait for me," the thin man told the taxi driver. When Jessie reached him, he repeated, "Where is your grandfather? I must speak to him!"

"He's not here," said Jessie. "But he should be back soon. Our housekeeper, Mrs. McGregor, is here."

The thin man shook his head impatiently. "She won't do. She won't do at all!"

He looked around the Aldens' yard. Then he stopped. He stared. A smile lit up his face. The ends of his mustache seemed to quiver like the whiskers on a cat.

"Ahhhh," he said. "There she is!"

"Who?" Jessie looked around, expecting to see Mrs. McGregor or Violet. But she saw no one.

"An excellent, excellent specimen. A real collector's item. And I, little girl, am a collector!"

Jessie still didn't know what the man was talking about. "My name is Jessie," she said.

"Oh! Yes, er, Jessie. Jessie Alden, isn't it? I just saw your picture in the paper. I rushed right over."

The man began walking across the back-yard toward the boxcar.

Jessie went after him. "Wait a minute," she said.

The thin man walked on. Watch began to bark.

Henry looked out the door of the boxcar. "Shh, Watch," he said. He grabbed Watch's collar and held onto it.

But the man didn't seem to notice Watch or Henry. Or even Violet or Benny, who had also come to the door.

When he reached the boxcar, the man stopped. He reached into his coat pocket and took out a folded newspaper. It was the same newspaper that had their picture in it.

Holding up the newspaper, the man looked from the picture on the front page to the boxcar and back again.

"What are you doing?" asked Henry.

The man shook his head. "*Not* a very good picture, I'm afraid. Doesn't do justice to the subject at all!"

"I think we look good!" said Benny indignantly.

The man kept shaking his head. He ignored Benny. "Not a good picture at all."

Then his smile lit up his face. "But good enough for me to take notice," he said. "And that's the important thing."

He put the newspaper back in his pocket, and threw his arms out wide.

"This beautiful, beautiful boxcar!" he exclaimed. "I must have it. It must be mine!"

The Aldens were so surprised that no one spoke for a moment. Then Jessie stepped around in front of the thin man. He was still staring at the boxcar.

"Excuse me," she said. "But what *are* you talking about?"

The man lowered his arms. He smiled down at Jessie as if he had noticed her for the first time. "Pardon me," he said. "My name is Casey Chessy. I am a collector of trains."

"I have a train set," Benny said.

The man shook his head impatiently. "No, no, no. Not toy trains. *Real* trains. I collect real trains. . . . May I take a closer look at your boxcar?"

"Of course," said Henry. The Aldens watched as Mr. Chessy walked all around the boxcar. They stood aside as he climbed up on the stump they used for a front step and went inside.

Mr. Chessy rubbed his hands as he inspected the inside of the old wooden boxcar. He thumped on the walls and peered into the corners. He even examined the ceiling!

Then he sneezed. And sneezed again.

"Gesundheit!" said Benny.

Holding a handkerchief up to his nose as he climbed quickly out of the boxcar, Mr. Chessy said, "You have a very fine boxcar. It is a wooden one, and those are rather rare. The wooden ones had a nasty habit of catching on fire or getting smashed to bits. But this one is in surprisingly fine condition."

"Thank you," said Benny. "Do you know a lot about trains?"

"Certainly," said Mr. Chessy. He backed away from the boxcar and stopped. "I travel by train. In fact, I have my own special railroad car, an old caboose that I have fixed up. I take vacations in it."

"That sounds like fun," said Violet.

"My caboose and I arrived in Greenfield late yesterday," Mr. Chessy went on. "I went out for a stroll this morning and just happened to buy a copy of the local paper. And there it was. This boxcar!"

He rubbed his hands together again. Then he turned abruptly to Henry. "When did you say your grandfather would be home? I have something very, very important to say to him."

"He'll be home soon," said Henry.

Mr. Chessy nodded. "Well, I can wait. It's not every day I get a chance to buy an old boxcar in as good condition as this one."

"Buy our boxcar!" Jessie cried. "Is that what you are talking about?"

"Naturally," answered Mr. Chessy. "Why else would I be here? I told you I collected trains."

"Not our boxcar," said Henry firmly.

Mr. Chessy smiled. "Now, now, children, I'm sure your grandfather will be able to buy you a nice playhouse with some of the money I'm going to pay him for this boxcar."

"Our boxcar is not just a playhouse," said Jessie.

"And what has Grandfather got to do with it?" asked Henry. "It's not his boxcar. It is ours!"

"Yours?" Mr. Chessy didn't like hearing that. He thought for a moment. Then he said, "Well, I'm willing to pay you a great deal of money for your boxcar."

"It's not for sale," said Jessie.

"Not at any price," said Violet.

"Not even a million, trillion dollars," said Benny.

As each of them spoke, the smile faded from Mr. Chessy's face.

He looked from one to the other. "You are being very foolish children," he said.

"No, we're not," said Jessie. "We don't need lots and lots of money. We have everything we need right here with our grandfather."

"Foolish children," repeated Mr. Chessy. "You'll change your minds."

He reached into his pocket and pulled out a card. "This is my card," he said. "If you call this number, you can always reach me. I'll talk to you again soon."

"We won't change our minds," said Henry.

"You'll change your minds," said Mr. Chessy. "I will have your boxcar. I'll see to that, one way or the other!"

With that, he marched back to the waiting taxicab and rode away.

CHAPTER 2

A Strange Visitor

"He can't have our boxcar, can he?" asked Benny.

"No, Benny," said Jessie. "It's our boxcar and we're going to keep it!"

Henry clapped his hand to his forehead. "Oh, no! I almost forgot. We're supposed to go to the grocery store for Mrs. McGregor."

Putting the rather strange Mr. Chessy out of their thoughts for the moment, the children hurried into the house.

"You didn't forget, did you?" Mrs. McGregor teased.

Henry's cheeks turned red. "Well, not exactly," he said. He was glad when Benny spoke up.

"What are we going to get at the grocery store?" Benny asked. "Is it for dessert tonight?" He looked hopeful. Benny was always hungry.

"No, I've already made dessert for tonight, Benny," answered Mrs. McGregor. Her merry eyes twinkled. "But if you don't like apple pie, I might be able to make something else."

"Oh, no!" exclaimed Benny. "I *love* apple pie."

His brother and sisters laughed. Mrs. McGregor laughed, too. Then she bent over the kitchen table and wrote something else on her grocery list. She picked up the list and handed it to Henry.

Henry folded it and carefully put it in his pocket. He checked to make sure he had enough money for groceries.

Violet asked, "Are we shopping for our Founders' Day dinner already?"

Mrs. McGregor nodded. "That you are,"

she said. "I may not have to begin cooking it yet, but I want to start getting ready."

"It'll be like Thanksgiving," said Benny. "I'm going to get all my favorite foods at one time!"

The four children got their bicycles and rode to town with Watch trotting beside them on his leash. When they got there, the sidewalks and streets were very crowded. So they decided to walk their bicycles along the sidewalk and look in the windows until they got to the grocery store.

Suddenly, Jessie stopped. "Look," she said. "A parade!"

Henry stopped behind Jessie and read aloud from the sign posted in the window of the hardware store: " 'The Founders' Day Parade: A Parade to Celebrate the Founding of Greenfield. Come see the parade — or be in it.' "

"Wow," said Jessie. "That would be great, to be in a parade!"

"I don't know," said Violet. "Parades are fun to watch, too." Violet looked a little wor-

THE
FOUNDERS'
DAY
PARADE
Come see
the parade—
or
be in it.

ried at the idea of being in a parade. She was very shy.

"Let's at least find out about it," said Henry. "Then we can decide."

"How will we find out?" asked Benny.

"Let's ask inside the hardware store," suggested Jessie. They all went inside.

"Could you tell us more about the parade?" Henry asked the owner of the store.

"It's on the sign in your window," added Jessie.

The hardware store owner said, "Of course. In fact, I can tell you everything you need to know." She reached over to the counter and picked up a colorful folded piece of paper. "This flyer will tell you all about the parade and how to join it."

"Thanks!" Henry said.

"You're welcome," said the hardware store owner. "See you at the parade."

"Or in it!" said Benny.

The Aldens walked outside. Henry read from the flyer as they walked. He read about how to enter the parade by filling out the form on the back of the flyer and mailing it to the Greenfield Parade Committee. "We have to tell them our names and what we are going to do in the parade," Henry said. "They'll let us know when to meet and where. Anybody can be in the parade, but listen to this: 'Parade members are encouraged to choose a costume or build a float that reflects some part of the history of Greenfield,' " he read aloud.

The children were quiet for a moment. Then Violet said, "Costumes would be fun. I could make a beautiful purple costume." Purple was Violet's favorite color.

"But what kind of costume?" Jessie asked. "Greenfield is very old. We have to think of something that goes with the history of our town."

The children thought and thought all the way to the grocery store. But they couldn't come up with an idea. After they finished shopping and were headed home, Henry said, "I know! Before we decide on a costume, let's ask Grandfather what he thinks."

"That's a good idea," said Jessie.

Violet said, "We can ask him at dinner

tonight. But you know what else I think we should do? We should learn more about the history of Greenfield, too."

"That's right," said Jessie. "We'll have an idea for the parade before you know it!"

"Do you hear that, Watch?" Benny said. "We're going to be in a parade!"

"This apple pie is the best pie I ever ate," said Benny that night at dinner.

"You say that every time Mrs. McGregor makes apple pie," said Grandfather Alden to his youngest grandchild.

"It's true every time," said Benny.

"Mrs. McGregor said that the apples came from an old apple orchard right here in Greenfield," said Violet. "She said they've been growing apples there for years and years."

"Farmers have been growing apples in and around Greenfield ever since I was a boy," said Grandfather.

"Will you tell us more about Greenfield?" asked Henry. He reached in his pocket and pulled out the flyer. "We got this at the hardware store today."

Mr. Alden read it, then looked up. "I don't suppose you want to be in the parade, do you?"

"Yes!" answered Jessie. "That's exactly what we want to do. But we have to think of the perfect costumes. Something historic."

"If you tell us more about Greenfield," explained Henry, "then maybe it will help us think of an idea for the parade."

So Grandfather Alden told his grandchildren all he knew about the history of Greenfield. He told them that when his own father was growing up, there was no electricity, and no running water in any of the houses. "When your great-grandmother was a girl about your age, Jessie, her job was to bring in water from the well. She knew how to make candles so the family would have light. And she knew how to drive a horse and carriage, because back then they didn't have cars."

"Did they have bicycles?" asked Benny.

"No bicycles either," said Grandfather. "Not until she was older. But they did have trains. The Greenfield Train Station is closed now. But in the old days it was the center of activity. I remember going there when I was a boy to watch the trains."

"What happened to the trains?" Jessie asked.

"There aren't as many as there used to be. Now people use trucks and cars," said Grandfather. "The trains only stop in the big towns. They still go through Greenfield, on the tracks by the old station at the edge of town, but they don't stop here anymore."

Jessie frowned. She was thinking hard. Suddenly she said, "Trains *are* a part of the history of Greenfield, aren't they? Just like it said in the newspaper about our boxcar?"

"They sure are," said Grandfather.

Jessie looked around the table. "I have an idea for the parade. Can you guess what it is?"

Everyone shook their heads. Jessie said, "I'll give you a hint. Once upon a time, four orphans and a little lost dog who didn't have any place to live went to live in a special place. And then their grandfather, who had been looking and looking for them, found them . . ."

"In an old, abandoned boxcar in the woods," said Violet. She slipped her hand into her grandfather's and continued the story. "So the four children went to live with their grandfather in a big, white house in Greenfield. And as a surprise . . ."

Henry finished, "Their grandfather brought the boxcar to the backyard of the house for his grandchildren. And their names were . . .

"Benny, Jessie, Violet, Henry, and Watch Alden," Benny burst out.

It was all true. That was how the Boxcar Children had come to live with their grandfather, James Alden.

Benny looked puzzled. "What does our boxcar have to do with the parade?"

"I think I know," said Henry. "Our boxcar is an old boxcar. Boxcars were probably part of the trains that once went through Greenfield. That means it's a part of Greenfield's history."

"That's right," said Jessie. "So, we should take our boxcar to be in the parade!"

"That's a great idea, Jessie," said Violet. She frowned. "But how will we get the boxcar in the parade? It doesn't have a motor!"

"I think I can help you with that," said Grandfather. "My old truck can pull the boxcar. I can hitch the boxcar to it and drive the truck in the parade."

"I can wear my engineer's costume with the red bandanna!" Benny said excitedly.

"Yes," said Henry. "And we can paint the boxcar and polish it and make it look extra special."

"We'll start first thing tomorrow," said Jessie.

For the rest of the night, the Aldens made plans to decorate the boxcar and to make costumes for the parade. Then they went to bed so they could get up early to mail their entry into the Founders' Day Parade and start getting their boxcar ready for the big day.

CHAPTER 3

Mr. Chessy's House

The next day, as soon as they had finished breakfast, the four Aldens helped Mrs. McGregor pack lunches for them. Then they got on their bicycles for a ride into Greenfield.

Watch wanted to come, but he couldn't. "We are going to the post office and then to the library, Watch," Benny explained. "We might be in the library for a long time. And dogs aren't allowed in the post office *or* the library."

Watch tilted his head. He couldn't understand why he wasn't allowed to go.

"I know, Watch," said Benny. "I think they should change those rules, too. But you can stay here with Mrs. McGregor until we get back."

Mrs. McGregor, who was standing by the back door, opened it and said, "I think I might have a nice dog biscuit in the kitchen for Watch."

At the word "biscuit" Watch got up and trotted happily into the house.

The Aldens set off for the post office. On the way, they stopped by to pick up their cousin, Soo Lee. Soo Lee lived with their cousins, Joe and Alice, in an old gray-shingled house nearby. The Boxcar Children had helped their cousins fix up the house when they moved there.

Soo Lee was waiting for them. She got on her bicycle as soon as her four cousins came into sight, and coasted down the driveway to join them.

The five children went to the post office first, to mail the parade entry form to the

Greenfield Parade Committee. Then they went to the library to research their costumes for the parade.

They found lots of books about trains and costumes in the old days. But the long dresses with their high necks and tight sleeves didn't look like much fun to Jessie or to Violet.

"These are pretty dresses," said Jessie. "But you can't run or play or even ride bicycles in them."

Violet agreed. "They don't look very comfortable, either. And I think it would be hard to make costumes to look like that."

"Listen to this," said Henry. "This book says that a train engineer usually wore a gray-striped cap and a red bandanna around the neck. And here's an old picture of an engineer on an early locomotive. He's wearing overalls, too."

The four children crowded around Henry to look at the picture.

"We all have overalls," said Jessie. "We could get caps and bandannas and all dress like engineers. They sell all kinds of caps and

bandannas at the department store in town, and they aren't too expensive. We can buy our costumes there and then we will have plenty of money left over for our other supplies."

"Look at this." Soo Lee pointed to another picture in the book. "We can learn some of the train signals, too. The signal for the train to stop is two arms up."

After doing a little more research on the history of Greenfield — and on railroads in particular — the children decided it was time for lunch.

"Let's take our lunches to the old railroad station," said Violet as they came out of the library.

When they got to the train station, the windows were all boarded up, the paint was chipped and peeling, and there was a big lock on the door.

"It looks like it could use some fixing up," said Henry. "But it would take a lot more than just paint!"

The five children took out their lunches and sat on stone steps that led up to the station. "I bet this was a really busy place a long time ago," Soo Lee said, as she took a big bite of her sandwich.

Just then, a voice said, "So! I was right. You changed your minds!"

The Aldens all looked up. It was Mr. Chessy!

"What are you doing here?" exclaimed Henry in surprise.

"This is where I'm staying." Mr. Chessy swung around and motioned with his hand. Then the Aldens saw an old-fashioned railroad car pulled off onto a side track near the back of the train station. "That's my traveling home," the man said. "It's an old caboose."

"It looks a little like our boxcar," said Henry.

"The first cabooses were just the last boxcars on the trains, you know." Mr. Chessy sounded almost friendly.

Benny cried, "I'd like to see what your boxcar looks like!"

Mr. Chessy looked surprised — and pleased. "Would you?" he asked. "Come along and I'll show you the inside."

The children all looked at one another. "Thank you!" said Henry.

The children had finished lunch. They quickly cleaned up and followed Mr. Chessy to his railroad car.

"Come in, come in," said Mr. Chessy. He stepped back and motioned for them to come into his caboose.

The Aldens couldn't help thinking of how they'd made their boxcar a home when they'd first lived in it. Their boxcar had an old table they'd found, with a blue tablecloth on it. They'd made beds at one end out of pine needles. They didn't have any light, except when they built a fire outside to cook.

But this caboose had a lamp that looked like an old-fashioned lantern. It had a stove and a refrigerator and even a sink with a little window above it.

Mr. Chessy proudly showed them around his caboose, explaining how he had designed and built everything himself.

Then he opened a narrow door. He stepped inside — and disappeared!

"Come on up!" his voice said above them.

A short ladder was inside the door. The children climbed up it, and found themselves in a small square room with windows all around and benches around all the walls.

"This is the cupola, or crow's nest," said Mr. Chessy. "Conductors and trainmen sat here to watch the train — and the scenery! I'm glad you came to see my little home. I'd take just as good care of your boxcar, if you should ever decide to sell it, you know. I'll be leaving soon, but you have my card — if you change your minds."

"Thank you," said Henry, without saying anything about selling the boxcar. The others thanked him, too.

Mr. Chessy was smiling as they left. When Jessie looked over her shoulder, however, she saw Mr. Chessy wasn't smiling anymore. He had his arms folded and his eyes were narrowed.

Was Mr. Chessy just pretending to be nice because he wanted their boxcar? she wondered.

But Jessie didn't say anything. She just listened as her brothers and sister told Soo

Lee all about Mr. Chessy and his offer the day before to buy the boxcar. They didn't have to tell her that they'd never, ever sell it. Soo Lee knew that already!

They decided to go to the hardware store next to get supplies for fixing up the boxcar, and then to the department store.

When they got to the hardware store, the owner remembered the Aldens from their last visit. "Did you enter the parade?" she asked.

"We sure did," said Benny. "We're going to be engineers in our boxcar."

The owner of the hardware store, like many people in Greenfield, knew the story of the Boxcar Children. She nodded approvingly. "That's a neat idea."

Henry explained that they were going to paint the boxcar for the parade and soon the Aldens had almost more supplies than they could carry.

After that, they went to the department store and bought red bandannas and engineer's caps. They even bought an extra bandanna for Watch to wear.

It was getting late. They quickly loaded the supplies on their bicycles, and headed for home.

"I don't think we're going to have time to start fixing the boxcar today," said Henry.

"I've got to go home," said Soo Lee. "Tomorrow I can't help you. But I'll come over as soon as I can the day after." They rode with Soo Lee back to her house. As she went inside, she waved her new engineer's cap at her cousins. "See you day after tomorrow!" she called.

That evening at dinner, the children told Grandfather all about their busy day. They also told him about visiting Mr. Chessy's railroad car.

"Mr. Chessy. Hmmm. I was thinking about what you told me and remembered I'd read an article about him in a magazine recently. I imagine he could tell you all about the history of your boxcar."

"I don't think he will want to talk to us about anything except selling our boxcar," said Jessie.

Grandfather laughed. "Collectors like to talk about the things they collect. He might be willing to talk to you."

"Then maybe we can call him tomorrow." Henry yawned. "But not tonight. Tonight I am too tired."

Everyone agreed that it had been a long day, but a good one, and that they could hardly wait for tomorrow.

CHAPTER 4

Sam and Susie

The Boxcar Children got up early the next morning, ate a big pancake breakfast, and hurried out to the boxcar to begin work. They were going to repaint the whole outside of the boxcar a beautiful bright red.

"First we need to sand the floors and the walls and all the rough spots," said Henry. "We can sand off the old paint and put new paint on."

"That sounds like a lot of work," said Benny. Benny liked to work hard.

"It will be a lot of work, Benny. But think of how good our boxcar will look," said Violet.

The Aldens went to work on the boxcar while Watch slept in the sun on the old stump. They hadn't been working long, however, before they had visitors. It was Mr. Chessy and Grandfather!

"But we didn't call you yet!" exclaimed Benny in surprise as Mr. Chessy walked across the grass toward them.

"After I saw you yesterday, I couldn't stop thinking about the boxcar," said Mr. Chessy. He turned to Mr. Alden. "So I took the matter to Mr. Alden. I . . . ah . . . ah . . . achoo!" He sneezed, looked at Watch and frowned. Then he went on. "As I hoped, your grandfather understood the generosity of my offer. And that I was the one who would give such a fine boxcar a proper home."

The Aldens were puzzled.

Mr. Chessy held up his hand. "In short, I've made my offer to your grandfather. I knew he would see things my way."

The children were shocked. Had Grandfather sold their boxcar? Before they could speak, Mr. Alden said, "Yes. Mr. Chessy came to me with a very generous offer. I suggested we walk out here to tell you."

Mr. Alden turned to Mr. Chessy. "But, the boxcar belongs to my grandchildren. If they don't want to sell it, then it's fine with me."

"Hooray for Grandfather!" Benny burst out.

Mr. Chessy said, "What! I don't believe this! You are going to regret your decision, mark my words! I don't give up so easily. I'll be back!"

Then he stomped away just as he had the last time he'd visited.

"I guess he won't be telling us about the history of the boxcar," Henry said.

Grandfather shook his head. But he didn't say anything. Instead he inspected the work that everyone had done and admired it. Then he went back into the house.

"What a strange man Mr. Chessy is," said Violet. "We would never sell our boxcar. Why can't he understand that?"

"Well, at least it didn't do him any good

to try to be sneaky," said Jessie.

"I'm glad," said Benny. "Because I want to ride on it in the parade."

"Then we'd better get back to work," said Henry.

The children worked all morning. Just when it was time to take a break, they heard a familiar bell ringing from the street.

"It's Sam! Sam and Susie!" said Benny excitedly. He put down his sandpaper and ran toward the sound.

During the warm weather, Sam and his Clydesdale horse, Susie, drove around Greenfield and sold ice cream and soda and treats from the wagon. Business was so good that during the winter, Susie got to rest in the warm barn while Sam made beautiful furniture that people ordered.

The other three Aldens followed Benny. Sure enough, Sam stood there beside his big old wagon. Susie was hitched to the front. Susie, who was big and brown with a golden mane and tail, a white star on her forehead, and one white front foot, lowered her head. She and Watch were sniffing noses.

Sam's old wagon was more like a house on wheels. "It's not as fast or fancy as a trailer or a truck," Sam liked to say, "but it gets me there just the same."

"You should have your wagon in the parade," Benny was saying as Henry, Jessie, and Violet came up.

"The Greenfield Founders' Day Parade?" asked Sam. "Now that's an idea. But if I'm not in the parade, you can be sure Susie and I will be there, selling hot chocolate and sodas and maybe even some ice cream if it's not too cold."

"It's not too cold for ice cream today, is it?" asked Benny.

"No," said Jessie. "We can have some. But just a little. It's almost time for lunch."

"I hope our boxcar is as nice as your wagon when we have finished fixing it up for the parade," Henry said.

"I'm sure it will be," said Sam, who had seen the Aldens' boxcar before. "If I didn't have this wagon, Susie and I would be proud to drive such a fine boxcar!"

"It's a beautiful wagon," said Violet softly.

She admired the wagon very much. A little table folded out of one wall and a little bed out of the other.

The Aldens paid Sam for their ice cream and went back to work. They worked on the boxcar right up through lunch. After lunch they were ready to begin painting.

They painted until dinnertime — and until they ran out of paint.

"We'll get some more tomorrow," said Henry. "And I think we should get some polish for the handles and the hinges on the door of the boxcar."

"It looks great," said Jessie. "But it is going to look even better!"

Tired and pleased with all the work they'd done, the Aldens went in for dinner. They talked about Sam and Susie, and about Mr. Chessy.

"Sam is nice," said Violet. "But I don't like Mr. Chessy."

"Well, he won't get our boxcar," said Jessie. "There's nobody in the world that could get our boxcar, so don't worry, Violet!"

CHAPTER 5

The Tantrum

Henry, Jessie, Violet, Benny, and Soo Lee were coming out of the hardware store the next morning with more paint and supplies for the boxcar, when a voice said, "Hush, Becky. If you're good, I'll ask these nice children to tell you about their boxcar. Remember? You saw their picture in the newspaper this morning!"

The Aldens turned to see a young woman holding the hand of a little girl with golden curls and blue eyes. The little girl was wearing a pink dress with a big white sash, lacy

41

pink tights, and white shoes with silver buckles. She was wearing a pink coat that exactly matched her dress.

"Oh! How pretty you look!" exclaimed Violet. "Just like a picture in a magazine."

"Say thank you, Becky," said the young woman.

Becky pushed out her lip and pouted.

"This is Becky Jennings and I'm her baby-sitter, Martha. We saw your picture in the newspaper with the article about the parade," Martha went on. "It was a very nice picture, wasn't it, Becky?"

Becky still didn't say anything.

"Thank you, " said Henry.

"Becky liked your boxcar, didn't you Becky?"

Suddenly Becky's face turned very red. Her eyes screwed shut. Then she began to scream!

"I want it!" she screamed. "Mine, mine, mine! My boxcar! I want the boxcar! MINE. GIVE IT TO ME!"

Everyone was so shocked that they didn't know what to do.

Becky jerked her hand out of her baby-
sitter's hand. Then she flung herself down
on the ground and began to kick her heels
and pound her fists in the dirt. "MINE.
OOOOH!" she wailed.

Suddenly, she didn't look like a picture in
a magazine anymore.

Martha's cheeks burned with embarrass-
ment. She bent over and picked Becky up.
"Stop that!" she pleaded.

Becky screamed louder. Martha turned
and began to carry the screaming child away.
"I'm sorry about this," she called over her
shoulder to the Aldens. "It was nice meeting
you. . . ."

As she left, the Aldens heard her say,
"Becky! Stop screaming! Your father will
buy you a nice, new playhouse of your own!
You don't need the boxcar! He'll . . . he'll
buy you your own boxcar for a playhouse!
You know he will. . . ."

The two disappeared around the corner as
the Aldens watched. Two women who were
standing nearby, and had seen the whole
thing, shook their heads in disapproval, and

a short man with a plaid jacket just stared after Becky and her baby-sitter.

One of the women sniffed loudly. "Well," she said. "Mr. Harold Jennings may be one of the richest men in Greenfield. But all that money and that fancy house on Mansion Road hasn't given his daughter good manners!" The two women walked away.

Jessie said, "What a spoiled girl!"

"I'm glad she's not my sister!" said Benny.

"Or my cousin!" said Soo Lee.

Still shaking their heads in amazement, the Aldens hurried home.

They'd just reached the hill near their house when Henry stopped and pointed. "Look!" he said.

Down below, at the bottom of the hill, stood Susie. She was wearing her harness, but she wasn't pulling the wagon. She kept shaking her mane and snorting as if she was upset.

"What happened to Sam? Where is his wagon?" said Violet in a worried voice. Then her eyes widened. "Oh, no!" she exclaimed.

The others gasped. They'd seen it, too.

Sam's wagon had crashed against a tree at the bottom of the hill. It was in what seemed like millions of pieces. One of the wheels lay in the road. Ice cream was melting on the sidewalk.

Just then, Sam came out into the road from the bushes where he had gone to pick up another wheel. He looked up and saw the Aldens and waved.

They hurried to the bottom of the hill.

"Sam! What happened?" asked Jessie.

Sam shook his head. "I'm not sure. We were just going up the hill when somehow the wagon got loose and slid right back down! I've never seen anything like it. I'm lucky I wasn't in it — and that Susie wasn't hurt!"

"Can you fix it?" asked Henry.

Again Sam shook his head. "Don't know if I can," he said. "But I'm sure gonna try." He looked sadly around at the pieces of his wagon and at the melting ice cream. "I'm trying to gather up as much stuff as I can to take home. Then I'll come back with my truck to get the rest."

"We'll help you,' said Henry.

"Of course," said Jessie.

The children helped Sam gather up some of his belongings while he tied a few of the bigger items from the wagon on Susie's back. Then, holding Susie's bridle, Sam led the way to his home. They put everything in the red barn behind Sam's house.

"After I get Susie out of her harness and settled into her stall in the barn here, I'll go get the rest of the wagon pieces," said Sam. "I appreciate your help."

"Don't worry, Sam. You'll be able to fix your wagon," said Soo Lee.

"Maybe," said Sam. But he didn't sound as if he believed it.

The last thing the children saw as they left was Sam standing in front of the barn, holding the wheel of the wagon and shaking his head sorrowfully.

"Time for me to go," said Soo Lee, late that afternoon. She sighed. "I wish I could have finished."

"We didn't expect to finish today, Soo

Lee," said Henry. "Don't worry. We're almost done and we've got plenty of time before the parade."

"I'll see you tomorrow," said Soo Lee. She got on her bicycle and pedaled away.

The Aldens began putting away the paint and washing the paintbrushes. Watch, who'd been sleeping inside the boxcar under the table, came to the door and barked. He was hoping that now it was time to play.

Benny picked up a stick. "Here boy! Catch!" Watch jumped out of the boxcar and he and Benny began to play a game of catch-the-stick.

"What a smart little dog!" said a man's voice.

Jessie was so startled that she jumped up. "Who are you?" she blurted out to the short, slight man who was standing there. He had on a plaid jacket and brown pants, and had three thin strands of brown hair combed over a bald spot on the top of his head. His nose was long and red at the end.

Watch heard how surprised Jessie sounded and stopped playing catch with Benny. He ran over to stand beside Jessie. He lowered his head and growled at the man.

"Good dog! Nice dog!" said the man. "Er, I'm sorry if I scared you. My name is, er, Ralph. Ralph Winters. I, er . . ." Ralph stopped and looked at Watch nervously. "He's not going to bite me, is he?"

"No," said Jessie. Then she added honestly, "At least, I don't think he is."

Watch stopped growling. But he still watched Mr. Winters carefully.

Just then Henry and Violet came out of the boxcar.

Jessie introduced them to Mr. Winters.

Still glancing at Watch, Mr. Winters nodded. "I'm glad to meet you all. I wondered if you could help me?" he said.

"We will if we can," said Violet.

"It's about your boxcar," said Mr. Winters. "I saw the article in the paper and I want to buy it!"

"Oh, no!" Benny cried. "Did Mr. Chessy send you!"

Now it was Mr. Winters' turn to be surprised. "Mr. Chessy? Who is Mr. Chessy?"

he asked. "I represent Senator Teacher. She is running for office and she wants to use your boxcar as part of her campaign!" Mr. Winters threw out his arms as if he were making a wonderful announcement.

The four children stared at him in disbelief. Henry finally said, "Our boxcar's not for sale."

"Oh, but wait until I tell you about it," said Mr. Winters eagerly. "She's conducting an old-fashioned whistle-stop tour. That means that she is going to ride the train from town to town and make speeches from the back of the last car on the train, just like President Harry Truman did in 1948. The car will be specially designed with a platform attached to the back for her to stand on. Your boxcar would be perfect — with a little redesigning, of course."

Mr. Winters rubbed his hands together. He licked his lips. His eyes shifted nervously from side to side. "What do you think?" he asked. "Are you going to help Senator Teacher?"

"I'm sorry," said Henry firmly. "We'd like

to help you. But the boxcar isn't for sale —
at any price."

"Please! Just think about it!" cried Mr.
Winters. "Here's my business card at the senator's offices in Greenfield. Like I said, think
about it and give me a call."

"We have thought about it," said Benny.
"Lots. And we've said 'no' lots, too."

"Thank you for your offer," said Jessie
firmly. "Good-bye."

Suddenly Mr. Winters looked angry. "It's
very selfish of you not to want to help," he
said. He turned around and stomped away.

"Good grief," said Jessie. "Can you believe
it?"

"He was not a nice man," said Benny. "He
was mean. I didn't like him and Watch didn't
like him. We're glad he went away."

At that, Jessie had to laugh. "We are, too,
Benny. Now let's go get ready for dinner.
We have a lot more work to do tomorrow on
our boxcar!"

It rained the next morning, but in the
afternoon the Aldens got back to work. The

first coat of paint had dried and it was time to put on a second coat.

After they gave the boxcar its second coat of paint, they would have to paint the trim. The floor needed sanding and the metal parts needed polishing.

Meanwhile, Mrs. McGregor was planning the special Founders' Day dinner. The Aldens were going to be in the parade in the morning on Founders' Day. Then they were going to come home and have their special dinner that afternoon.

For several days the Aldens worked hard on their boxcar. They began to worry that they wouldn't finish in time for the parade.

But they did. At last the wood of the boxcar was smooth from sanding, and shiny with new paint. All the rusty metal hinges and latches had been polished until they shone. The wheels had been oiled so that they would turn smoothly and the spokes of the wheels had been painted, too. It was hard work, but the Aldens loved seeing the old boxcar look so shiny and new. They were very proud of it.

"I knew we would finish with plenty of time for the parade," said Henry, smiling.

Violet clasped her hands together. "It looks wonderful."

"Let's get Grandfather," said Jessie. She and Henry went to get Grandfather Alden.

When they came out, they all stood in front of the boxcar except Watch. He sat proudly inside, his ears up and his tail wagging. He seemed to know how special the boxcar looked.

"You've done a wonderful job," said Grandfather. "You'll be the stars of the parade."

"Our boxcar will!" said Henry. Everyone was very pleased. It would be good, however, to take a few days off from working on the boxcar, before it was time for the parade.

Benny gave the boxcar a pat as he left. "See you tomorrow, old boxcar," he said. Then he followed his brother and sisters and Grandfather into the house for dinner.

CHAPTER 6

Missing!

"Benny, you haven't finished your breakfast yet," said Jessie.

"Watch hasn't eaten his at all," said Benny. He pointed to Watch's bowls in the corner of the kitchen by the door. One was full of water. The other was full of dog food.

"He's probably out digging holes," said Henry. "He'll come in when he's hungry."

"Why don't you finish your cereal?" Jessie said. "Then you can go call Watch."

Quickly Benny began to eat. He ate all his

breakfast, then raced out the back door to call Watch.

A few minutes later Benny ran back in. His face was pale. His eyes were wild. He waved his hands and didn't seem to be able to speak.

"Benny! What's wrong?" exclaimed Henry, jumping out of his chair so fast it turned over.

"Gone!" Benny managed to say at last. "Gone! Gone!"

"Oh, Benny, don't worry. Watch didn't go far. We'll find him," said Violet.

Benny shook his head.

"Calm down," Jessie said. She put her arm around her younger brother's shoulders. "What's wrong?"

Benny took a deep breath. He looked around at everybody. Then he said, "The boxcar! It's *gone*!"

"Gone? Benny, are you sure?" gasped Violet.

Benny nodded. "I'm sure, and Watch is gone, too!"

He turned and ran back out the door. His brother and sisters raced after him.

They ran toward where the boxcar had been.

They stopped and stared.

The boxcar *was* gone. Only the stump they'd used as a front step remained.

Jessie's mouth dropped open. Violet put her hand over her mouth. Henry rubbed his eyes as if he couldn't believe what he was seeing.

"See?" said Benny, pointing at where the boxcar had once stood.

"Where could a boxcar go?" whispered Violet. "It couldn't just disappear!"

"Someone must have taken it," said Jessie. "But how?"

Henry pointed down at the ground. "Look!" Big, wide, muddy ruts cut through the grass. "Someone must have pulled it away."

"We can follow the tracks!" said Jessie. The children ran in the direction of the muddy ruts. But the tracks stopped at the road.

Benny sat down and covered his face.

Violet knelt down beside him. "Don't cry, Benny. It'll be all right. We'll find the boxcar."

Benny lifted his face to look at Violet. "But the boxcar is gone. Even worse, Watch is gone, too."

"We'd better find Watch right away," said Henry. "Then he can help us look for the boxcar."

Benny felt more cheerful at the thought of this. They called and called, but Watch didn't come.

"Where could Watch be?" asked Jessie at last.

"He'll come back," said Henry.

"I didn't let him in the house last night," said Benny in a worried tone of voice. "I went to bed early. I thought someone else would."

"I didn't let him in," said Violet.

Jessie and Henry shook their heads. They hadn't either.

"But maybe Grandfather or Mrs. Mc-Gregor did," said Henry. "And then let him out early this morning."

The Aldens went back in the house to tell Mrs. McGregor and Grandfather. They ran outside to see for themselves.

They couldn't believe that the boxcar was missing. Grandfather shook his head. He frowned. "This is very serious," he said.

"We are going to find the boxcar," said Jessie, putting her hands on her hips. "And Watch. Don't worry."

"I know you've solved many mysteries," Grandfather Alden told his grandchildren. "But you've never had a mystery like this one. Who would steal a boxcar? And why would Watch run away for a whole night? Because if he had been here, he would have barked when someone took the boxcar."

"I don't know. But we'll figure it out," said Henry.

The four Aldens went back out to where the boxcar had been. They searched the entire area for clues. They weren't sure what they were looking for, but they didn't find anything that helped — not even a muddy footprint, or dog's paw print.

"What do we do now?" asked Benny.

Henry put his hand on his chin and thought. Then he said, "Mr. Chessy!"

"What?" Benny said, confused.

"That's right!" exclaimed Jessie. "Mr. Chessy. Remember how badly he wanted to buy our boxcar? He was very unhappy when we wouldn't sell it to him. He said he'd get it one way or the other."

"I thought he would come back. He was *so* angry. But he never did," said Violet.

"Maybe he never came back because he didn't want us to get suspicious," said Jessie. "Maybe he realized we would never sell the boxcar to him, so he took it!" She jumped up. "We have to go talk to Mr. Chessy right away."

"But he said he was leaving soon, remember?" said Henry. "What if he took our boxcar and left town?"

"What about Watch?" asked Benny. "We should look for Watch!"

"We'll leave a bowl of Watch's favorite food outside on the steps for him," said Henry. "We can ask Mrs. McGregor and

Grandfather to look out for him in case he comes home."

"We'll call for Watch and look for him on our way to Mr. Chessy's," Jessie said.

"But what if we don't find him?" Benny cried. "What if he's lost?"

"If he still hasn't come home when we get back," said Henry, "we'll go the animal shelter and to Dr. Scott's and tell them Watch is missing. We'll put up signs at the shelter and at the veterinarian's, too. Then we'll put up signs all over town, and offer a reward."

"Don't forget, we solved the mystery of the missing cat," said Violet. "We found her — and we found the champion dog from the dog show when she disappeared."

Benny felt a little better when he remembered that. Slowly he nodded. "We *will* find Watch," he said, getting up off the stump. "And our boxcar."

Benny put down a big bowl of Watch's favorite food by the back steps of the house. He told Grandfather Alden and Mrs. McGregor to watch out for the little dog. Then the Aldens got on their bicycles and pedaled as fast as they could into Greenfield and to the old train station.

"Look, Mr. Chessy's train car is still there!" shouted Jessie.

"I'm so glad," said Violet.

"Let's ask Mr. Chessy some questions and see how he acts," suggested Henry. "We won't tell him our boxcar is missing."

Everyone agreed that Henry's plan was a good one. They parked their bicycles, and went up to Mr. Chessy's caboose. They walked up the stairs that had been lowered from the edge of the caboose beneath the door. Henry knocked loudly on the door.

Mr. Chessy slid the door open at once. He seemed surprised to see the Aldens. He stroked his mustache and raised his eyebrows. "Well, well, well," he said. "What have we here?"

"Hello, Mr. Chessy," said Henry politely.

Mr. Chessy answered, "Has your grandfather managed to make you change your minds about selling me the boxcar?"

"Not exactly," said Jessie. She frowned. If Mr. Chessy had stolen the boxcar, would he still ask them if they wanted to sell it?

"Well," said Mr. Chessy, folding his arms. "I think it is a disgrace. That boxcar should be in a museum. Or a collection like mine, where it can be properly cared for. Dragging it up and down the streets in a parade! Hmmmph!"

"If you bought our boxcar," asked Violet, "would you pull it away with a truck?"

Mr. Chessy looked shocked. "Certainly not!" he said. "I would have a special truck and lift the boxcar onto it. That would be the safest way for it to travel."

"Wouldn't you take it to a railroad track and pull it home with you?" asked Benny.

"Young man," said Mr. Chessy, "there is no way I would treat a valuable old boxcar like that!"

"But what about your own railroad car that you travel in?" asked Henry.

Mr. Chessy twisted his mustache. His eyes shifted. Then he said, "Well, I suppose it doesn't hurt to tell you the truth. My caboose is not exactly a real railroad car. It's a replica. A special, exact full-sized replica of the real thing. I never could find a real caboose that was in good enough condition."

"Oh," said Benny. Then he said, "What's a replica?"

"It's a copy, Benny," explained Henry. He couldn't think of any more questions to ask Mr. Chessy. Neither could anyone else.

"Well, thank you," said Henry.

"Hmmph," said Mr. Chessy crossly.

As the Aldens left, Benny suddenly turned around. "You haven't seen our dog Watch, have you?" he called.

"Dog? Absolutely not!" Mr. Chessy suddenly sneezed. Then he slammed the door.

"Well, I guess it wasn't Mr. Chessy," said Jessie.

"But it could have been him," argued Henry. "He could have put it up on a truck and taken it away in the middle of the night."

"I bet Watch would have liked Mr. Chessy's caboose. He liked Sam and Susie's wagon," Benny said sadly.

Jessie looked over at Benny. "Mr. Chessy's caboose *was* like Sam and Susie's wagon, wasn't it Benny?" Her eyes narrowed. "I wonder . . ."

"What is it, Jessie?" asked Violet.

Jessie stopped in the middle of the sidewalk. "What if Sam did it?" she said. "What if Sam took our boxcar so he and Susie could have a new wagon?"

CHAPTER 7

Suspects

"Sam would *never* take our box-car!" cried Benny. "He and Susie are our friends!"

"I don't want to think he would either, Benny," said Henry. "But we have to check everything. And Sam's wagon is broken. He *did* say that our boxcar would make a great wagon."

"That's true," said Violet quietly.

No one said anything else the rest of the way home, except to call for Watch. When they got home, Benny dropped his bike and ran around to the back of the house to see if the dog food he'd left out was gone. The others quickly followed.

But the dog food was still there. Mrs. McGregor opened the kitchen door as they ran up the back steps.

"Has Watch come home?" asked Benny breathlessly.

Mrs. McGregor shook her head sadly. "The boxcar? Did you find it?" she asked.

"No," said Benny, his shoulders slumping with disappointment.

"It's a strange thing," said Mrs. McGregor. "Watch loved the boxcar as much as you do. He stayed there all the time. Slept in it sometimes during the day and more than once when I called him in at night, he'd come from that direction. I would think he'd be barking and barking if anybody came to steal it."

"Grandfather said that, too. He must have been gone already," said Henry.

"Watch is a smart dog," said Mrs. McGregor. "He'll find his way home. Time for lunch now."

But the Aldens didn't have very big appetites. They ate quietly. When they'd finished, Henry said, "We might as well keep busy. We'll keep looking for Watch. And we'll go visit Sam."

They called and looked for Watch as they headed for Sam's house. On the way, they stopped by the animal shelter and Dr. Scott, the veterinarian's. But no one had seen Watch.

When they reached Sam's house, they saw that Susie was out in the pasture. A blanket had been thrown over her back and her jaw moved slowly as she chewed on a wisp of hay.

Then Sam came out of the barn. When he saw the children riding up his driveway he quickly pulled the door of the barn shut. Then he locked it and walked out to meet them.

"Hello," Sam said.

"We came to see how your wagon is doing," said Jessie. "Have you fixed it yet?"

"Well, you can see that Susie is still out in the pasture," said Sam with a laugh. "That means I haven't fixed it yet, or she'd be hitched to it and we'd be out on the road."

"Can you fix it?" asked Violet.

"I'm not making any promises," said Sam. "But I haven't given up hope of having a fine wagon for me and Susie again someday soon."

The Aldens exchanged glances. Sam was being very vague. He wouldn't answer any of their questions "yes" or "no."

"Could we see the wagon?" asked Henry.

Sam said, "You don't want to see it. When I finish working on it, if I ever do, then you can. But you can go visit Susie. She'd be glad to say hello." Sam suddenly looked around. "Say, where is Susie's friend? That little dog of yours?"

"Watch is gone," said Benny. "He ran away last night."

"That's terrible! I'll look out for him," Sam said.

"We'll visit Susie another time," said Jessie quickly. "When Watch comes home, so he can visit, too. Thank you."

The Boxcar Children got on their bikes

and rode quickly back up the driveway. As soon as they were out of sight, Jessie pulled her bicycle into the bushes and stopped.

The others stopped, too.

Henry said, "Sam wouldn't let us in the barn. He's acting as if he's hiding something."

Jessie nodded. "That's what I think, too, Henry."

"Maybe we should watch him," said Benny.

"I think we should, too," said Jessie. "I think we should wait here and when Sam drives to town, we'll follow him!"

"But what about Watch?" asked Benny.

"You and I will go and keep looking for Watch," Violet said to Benny. To her older brother and sister she said, "We'll meet you back at the house in time for dinner."

After awhile, a battered gray truck pulled out of the farm's driveway. Sam drove by.

Quickly Henry and Jessie got on their bicycles and followed him. They had to pedal fast to keep him in sight.

First Sam stopped at the post office and bought some stamps. Then he stopped at the library and returned some books. Then he went to the pet supply shop — and bought a big bag of dog food!

Jessie grabbed Henry's arm. "Look!" she exclaimed, as Sam threw the dog food in the back of the truck. "Sam doesn't have a dog! Why is he buying dog food?"

"I know why!" Henry said. "And I know where Watch is!"

Jessie's eyes opened wide. She looked over at Sam, who was getting back into his truck. "Sam?" she whispered. "Sam has Watch?"

Henry said, "Yes." But before he could explain, Sam got in his truck and drove away. This time they couldn't keep up with him.

"It's o-okay," panted Henry, pulling his bicycle to a stop. "He's just going home, I think. And it is almost time for us to get home, too."

"Why would Sam take Watch?" asked Jessie.

"I don't think he *meant* to," said Henry.

"But I think Watch was asleep in the boxcar. When Sam took the boxcar, he closed the door and locked Watch inside. Now he's afraid to let him go because Watch will take us right back to his barn."

"You're right, Henry!" cried Jessie. "We'll keep a close eye on Sam and we'll find Watch and our boxcar."

"Yes," Henry agreed. "But first we have to go home and tell Violet and Benny what we found out."

When Henry and Jessie got home and told Violet and Benny what they thought had happened to Watch, the others didn't want to believe it. Neither did Soo Lee, who had come over to help Benny and Violet look for Watch.

But then Violet said, "Oh! That's why Watch didn't bark!"

"Why, Violet?" asked Soo Lee.

"Because he knows Sam and Susie!"

"Have we solved the mystery?" asked Benny.

"I think we *almost* have," said Henry. "It's

too late to go back now, but tomorrow we'll go out there again. We'll find Watch."

Early the next morning, Mrs. McGregor asked the Aldens to go pick up some more groceries for the Founders' Day dinner.

They decided that Henry and Violet would go to the grocery store, and Jessie and Benny would go to Sam's farm.

When Jessie and Benny got out to Sam's farm, they settled down to wait.

Meanwhile, Henry and Violet bought the groceries for Mrs. McGregor. They were just coming out of the store when Violet said, "Look. There's the little spoiled girl."

Sure enough, the young girl with the golden-blonde curls and the big blue eyes who had thrown a temper tantrum in front of the Aldens was walking down the sidewalk. She was holding the hand of a tall man in a gray flannel suit.

"Hello there," Henry said to Becky.

"Hi," Violet added softly.

The man holding Becky's hand said, "Are

these some friends of yours, Becky? You should say hello."

But Becky didn't say anything. She acted as if she didn't even know who they were. Instead she tugged on the tall man's hand. "Can we go now, Daddy?" she asked. "I want to go play in my *new* playhouse!" She gave Henry and Violet a smug look.

"Sure, princess," her father said.

"Don't you remember us?" asked Violet. "You were with your baby-sitter, Martha. You told us you saw our picture in the newspaper with — "

"Daddy, I want to goooo," wailed Becky, her blue eyes filling with tears.

"Sorry," Becky's father said to Henry and Violet. "I don't know why she's behaving this way." He picked Becky up and carried her over to a car that was sitting at the curb. He put her inside and then they drove away.

"Well, that wasn't very nice," said Violet. Violet was shy, but she would never, ever be rude. No one in her family had ever behaved that way.

"I know why she's acting like that," said Henry. "She's spoiled."

"I hope I never get spoiled," said Violet.

That made Henry smile a little. "Don't worry, Violet. You could never be that mean," he told her.

Violet grabbed Henry's arm. "Look! There goes Sam into the grocery store."

"I wonder if Jessie and Benny were able to keep up with him?" said Henry.

His question was answered a moment later as Jessie and Benny came pedaling up to the grocery store. "Henry, Violet, Sam's . . ." Jessie ran out of breath and pointed to the grocery store.

"We know," said Violet. "We saw him go in. You can rest now while he's inside. When he comes out we'll help you follow him."

Jessie and Benny didn't get to rest very long. Sam came out soon after, carrying a big bag of groceries. He put it in the back of the truck and drove away.

The Aldens quickly followed.

Sam drove toward his farm. But before he got there, he turned off and went down a narrow country road. Then he turned up a narrow dirt driveway to a small gray house with green shutters. He parked his truck out front as the Aldens ducked behind some trees.

They watched as Sam picked up the groceries and knocked on the front door of the house. Several minutes later, the door opened. A small, white dog came wriggling out and jumped up to put his paws on Sam's leg.

"Sam! Thank you for doing this," said a raspy voice. A man about Sam's age stepped out onto the porch. "My cold's going away, but I still feel pretty bad."

"Glad to help. Besides, after you gave me that old wagon of yours for parts to help put my wagon back together, it's the least I could do," said Sam. "Call me if you need anything else. I'll stop by tomorrow to visit . . . oh, wait. I just remembered something."

Sam ran back to his truck and grabbed the bag of dog food from the back. "I almost forgot this special delivery!" he said with a laugh, coming back up onto the porch.

The dog barked and the man coughed. Then the man said, "Thanks again, Sam. You're a good neighbor."

"My pleasure," said Sam. He waved and went back to his truck.

"Sam was buying dog food for his sick neighbor's dog, not Watch," Benny said. "He doesn't have Watch and our boxcar after all!"

CHAPTER 8

A Happy Reunion

"I guess so," admitted Henry.

Jessie thought for a moment. "But I still think Watch was in the boxcar when it was taken. Maybe we just couldn't hear him bark while he was locked inside."

"He would have barked at that mean Ralph man," said Benny.

"He sure would have, Benny," said Jessie, looking more hopeful. "Maybe Ralph Winters took the boxcar for the senator. And maybe he took Watch, too. All we have to do now is find Ralph Winters."

Violet was thinking hard, too. She said, slowly, "We saw that spoiled little girl again today. Becky. The one who wanted our boxcar. What about her?"

"How would she steal a boxcar?" asked Benny.

"I don't know," said Violet.

"I don't think she did it," said Henry. "How could she? She's just a little girl. But we'll keep her on our list of suspects. Right now, though, I think our best suspect is Ralph Winters. We need to find him."

Violet clasped her hands together. "Oh, no," she said. "What if Watch is still locked up in the boxcar? What if Mr. Winters doesn't even know he's there?"

It was too horrible to think about.

Jessie said quickly, "We still have Mr. Winters' business card at home. I put it in my desk drawer. We'll call him, and tell him our boxcar disappeared and we think our dog is locked inside. If Mr. Winters has the boxcar, he'll at least let Watch out. And you know Watch can find his way home!"

"Let's hurry!" cried Benny.

The children raced home. Jessie ran up to her room and came running back down the stairs, two at a time, a minute later.

"Here it is!" she said holding up the card triumphantly.

She hurried to the telephone and dialed the phone number on the card. "Hello?" she said. "May I please speak to Ralph Winters?"

Her eyes opened very wide as she listened. Then she said, "Oh, no! Are you sure? But . . . well, can you tell me where we could find him? It's very, *very* important. Maybe I could talk to Senator Teacher. She isn't? When will she be back? Oh." Jessie's voice grew very sad. "Oh. Thank you."

She put the phone receiver down slowly and stood there with her hands hanging at her sides.

"What is it?" Violet cried. "What's wrong?"

Jessie looked up at the other children. "Mr. Winters doesn't work for Senator Teacher anymore. He's been fired! And they wouldn't tell me where he lives so I could call him. They said they couldn't give out that information."

"We'll talk to the senator!" declared Henry.

"I tried. She wasn't there. They don't know when she'll be back to her office. She's out campaigning."

"We'll think of something," Henry said. "Don't worry."

But the children knew they had to solve the mystery and solve it soon — or they might never see Watch again!

That night Benny couldn't sleep. He got up and pressed his face against the window in his room and looked down into the backyard where the boxcar had stood.

The moon was out, and it was bright enough to see the stump that had been the step for the door of the boxcar.

Benny remembered how Watch could jump up into the boxcar without even using the stump as a step. He thought about how Watch had been all over Greenfield with the

Aldens while they were walking or riding their bicycles and even in the car. Watch was very smart. He could find his way home — Benny just *knew* it. But still he felt a little worried. His stomach even hurt a little.

Benny sighed. He was thinking about Watch so hard that he almost thought he could hear Watch barking.

Then Benny blinked. He blinked again. Something small and white was running by where the boxcar had been.

It *was* barking that Benny heard!

"Watch!" shouted Benny joyfully, jumping up and down. He didn't care that it was the middle of the night. "Watch!" he shouted as loudly as he could, running out of his room and down the stairs toward the back door. "Watch has come home!"

Doors slammed. Footsteps pounded in the hall. Everyone came running from their rooms. Mrs. McGregor came out with only one slipper on. Grandfather tied the sash around his robe as he ran.

Benny threw the back door open. A small furry body hit him and knocked him over.

"*WOOF,*" Watch barked, wild with excitement. "*Woof, woof, woof!*" He was wagging his tail so hard that his whole body shook. He licked Benny's face and his neck and his ears.

The kitchen light came on.

"Watch!" said Jessie. "You're back!"

Watch jumped up on her. He jumped up on Henry and Violet and Grandfather and Mrs. McGregor, too. He ran in circles around the kitchen. Everyone hugged him and kissed him and petted him and talked at once.

When everyone had calmed down a little, Grandfather said, "No one wanted dessert tonight after dinner this evening. Maybe now we should eat some ice cream to celebrate."

"Hooray!" said Benny, who was holding Watch. "Can Watch have some, too?"

"Yes," said Grandfather. "Watch can have some, too."

So the Aldens and Mrs. McGregor sat at the big kitchen table and ate vanilla ice cream in the middle of the night. And just that once, because it was a very special night,

Watch sat on Benny's lap and ate a little bit of ice cream out of a bowl of his very own.

They were all very happy. They were a whole family again, because Watch had come home.

"I wonder where you were, boy," said Henry to Watch the next morning. "I wish you could tell us. Do you know who took the boxcar?"

Watch licked Henry's hand.

"Are we ready?" asked Jessie.

They were going to Senator Teacher's office. They hoped that they could find out more about Mr. Winters.

"Yes," said Benny. He added, "And Watch is coming with us. We're not leaving him behind."

"Watch can come with us," said Henry. "A senator who doesn't like dogs shouldn't be elected, anyway!"

The Aldens and Soo Lee rode their bikes into Greenfield. Benny held Watch's leash and Watch trotted alongside him on the sidewalk.

The senator's office was a small two-story house near the town square. It was white with red-and-blue trim, and the United States flag and the state flag hung out front. There was also a big poster in the front yard with the senator's picture on it. It read: RE-ELECT SENATOR TEACHER.

The Aldens parked their bicycles and went inside. "We called yesterday afternoon," said Henry to the man behind the receptionist desk, who was flipping through a magazine. "About Ralph Winters."

The man looked up. "Ralph Winters." He shook his head. "Can't help you. He's gone. Fired."

"We have to find him," said Benny. "It's very important."

"Can't help you," said the receptionist, leaning back in his chair.

"But . . ." said Benny.

"Could we see Senator Teacher?" said Jessie. She was beginning to get angry.

"The senator is a very busy woman," said the receptionist. He unwrapped a stick of gum and began to chew it.

"*Woof!*" said Watch.

"Is that a dog?" The receptionist sat up. "Oh, no! Dogs aren't allowed!"

"You're a mean man!" said Benny, his face turning red.

"Not mean," a woman's crisp voice said. "Just not very smart sometimes."

Now it was the receptionist's face that turned red. "S-Senator Teacher," he said. "We weren't expecting you today."

"No, I didn't think you were," said the senator. She walked into the room. She was a short woman with close-cut silver hair. She had on a navy blue suit and navy blue shoes. She was wearing red earrings and a white blouse, and had red fingernails that matched her earrings.

The senator gave her receptionist a sharp look. "I'll talk to *you* later," she told him. Then she turned to the Aldens. "Come into my office. All of you. Let's see what I can do to help."

The Aldens followed the senator into her office. As fast as they could, they told her the whole story of the missing boxcar. When they finished, the senator shook her head.

"I'm sorry to disappoint you," she said. "I did discuss the idea of using a train with my staff — but Ralph Winters never mentioned your boxcar to me. And I've decided against using an actual train anyway. You see, the trains don't go enough places. So I'm going to have a large truck fixed up to look like a train, and that's what I'll use for my whistle-stop campaign."

"So Mr. Winters didn't have any reason to take our boxcar after all," said Henry.

"No," said the senator. "Not to my knowledge. And I don't know where Ralph is. He turned out to be very untrustworthy and I had to fire him. He was living in Silver City, but I don't know if he is still there."

"Thanks anyway," said Henry.

"I wish I could have helped you," said the senator. "Here."

She gave them campaign buttons and escorted them out of her office. "Come back if I can be of any help at all," she told them. She gave the receptionist another sharp look and added, "And bring your dog. I work for the voters and their families. Their *whole* families!"

"So Mr. Winters didn't take our boxcar," said Jessie as they left. "I don't think a senator would lie, do you?"

Henry said, "Not about stealing a boxcar!"

"I liked Senator Teacher," said Benny. "I'm going to vote for her when I grow up."

"I will, too, Benny," agreed Violet. "But we still haven't found our boxcar."

"We have to find it soon, or we can't be in the parade," said Henry. "Let's check on Mr. Chessy one more time."

The Aldens turned back down Main Street. But before they had gone very far, Watch pulled on his leash so hard that he almost pulled Benny over.

"Watch! Stop that!" scolded Benny.

Watch didn't listen. He strained on his leash and barked.

Someone shrieked. "I hate that nasty dog. He's barking at me again! Bad dog! Go away!"

It was Becky. She was walking with Martha.

The Aldens didn't stop to hear Becky shouting horrible things about Watch. Becky was very spoiled, but they were a little embarrassed because Watch was behaving badly, too.

"Watch, stop that!" Benny scolded again as they rode away. But it wasn't until they had turned the corner and Becky was out of sight that Watch stopped growling and barking and pulling on his leash.

"None of us likes her, Watch," said Henry. "You're a smart dog to know how mean she is right away, without ever even having met her."

"He's the smartest dog in the whole world," said Violet.

No one wanted to argue with that, especially since Watch was very good the rest of the way to Mr. Chessy's caboose.

"It's still here," said Violet.

They knocked on the door. Mr. Chessy smiled, just a little, when he slid open the door of his caboose and saw them standing there.

"Well, well, well if it's not the Boxcar Children. And just in time for a final visit. I'm getting ready to leave. Time to take my traveling railroad car home, you know. Have you changed your mind about your boxcar?"

Henry took a deep breath, "Even if we did change our mind, we couldn't sell it to you."

Mr. Chessy stopped smiling. "Why not?" he said.

"Because our boxcar is missing. It's been stolen!" said Jessie, watching Mr. Chessy closely.

"Stolen! But that's impossible!" Mr. Chessy seemed very surprised and shocked. Then Mr. Chessy sneezed. He took a big handkerchief out of his pocket and wiped his eyes.

"You don't have to cry about our boxcar," said Benny, even more surprised to see the tears in Mr. Chessy's eyes. "We'll find it."

With a sneeze, Mr. Chessy said, "I'm not. Although I am worried. Who would do such a terrible, terrible thing . . . achoo!"

"Oh. May we come in and see your caboose again?" Benny asked.

"No. No, no, no," Mr. Chessy shook his

head and wiped his eyes again. "In fact, I think I must ask you to leave."

"Leave? Why?" asked Henry.

Mr. Chessy waved his handkerchief in Watch's direction. Watch was sitting on the top step by Jessie.

"Because I'm very, very allergic to dogs. And even standing this close to your dog is making my eyes water and making me cough and snee . . . ah-*choo*."

"We'll leave right away," said Violet. The Aldens went quickly down the stairs.

"If you change your mind about selling your boxcar," Mr. Chessy called after them, "you know where to find me. . . ." Then the door of Mr. Chessy's traveling home closed.

"Allergic?" Benny asked. "Does being around any dogs in the world make him cough and sneeze?"

"Yes, it does," said Henry. "Let's walk our bicycles home. Watch looks as if he could use a rest from all the running with us he's been doing."

Hearing his name, Watch wagged his tail. The Aldens began to walk slowly home.

A horrifying thought came to Benny. "Oh! Does being allergic mean that Mr. Chessy can't have a dog ever?" he asked.

"I'm afraid so, Benny," said Violet.

"Poor Mr. Chessy," said Benny. "He'll never have a dog like you, Watch. Or any dog at all."

"Yes," said Jessie. She bent over and patted Watch's head and he wagged his tail again. "Mr. Chessy's boxcar is very nice, but it wouldn't be any fun to have the fanciest boxcar in the world if we didn't have Watch!"

CHAPTER 9

The Key to the Mystery

As the Aldens walked through Greenfield, they saw signs everywhere that said: COME TO THE GREENFIELD FOUNDERS' DAY PARADE! They saw shoppers hurrying about and children playing. Watch wagged his tail at the people passing by. He sniffed noses with a poodle on a leash.

"Everybody likes Watch," said Benny. "And Watch likes everybody." He paused and frowned. "Except Mr. Chessy doesn't like Watch. And Becky doesn't like Watch and Watch doesn't like Becky. And Watch doesn't like whoever took our boxcar. Do you, Watch?"

"Benny!" exclaimed Jessie. "That's it!"

"What?" said Benny.

"That's the key to the mystery!" said Jessie. She threw out her hands excitedly and almost dropped her bike.

"Whoa," said Henry, catching Jessie's bicycle before it fell over.

"Mr. Chessy couldn't have taken the boxcar because of Watch. He's too allergic to dogs to even let Watch near him. Remember how he had to jump out of the boxcar the day he visited it, because Watch was inside?"

"And he was sneezing then, too," Benny said.

"How does that help solve the mystery?" Henry asked.

"Well, when Watch saw Becky, he didn't like her. And she didn't like him. Remember what she said. 'I hate that nasty dog. He's barking at me again!' " Jessie went on. "But how did she know she didn't like 'that dog'? And how could Watch be barking at her 'again' if Becky and Watch had never met each other? At least, not when we were with Watch."

Violet said slowly, "But Becky acted as if she knew Watch. And Watch acted as if he knew Becky."

"And when we saw Becky, she said, 'I want to go play in my *new* playhouse.' Why did she say that about her new playhouse when she saw us?" asked Henry.

Everyone thought a moment. Henry continued, "She wanted our boxcar for her playhouse, remember? That's why seeing us reminded her of her playhouse . . . because our boxcar *is* her new playhouse!"

The Aldens all looked at one another. Then Jessie said, "And Watch was inside when she got it. That's why Watch doesn't like Becky. And why Becky doesn't like Watch!"

"But how could a little girl take a boxcar?" wondered Violet.

"I don't know, Violet. But we're going to find out where Becky Jennings lives. And I think when we do, we're going to find our boxcar!"

The Aldens looked up the name "Jennings" in the phone book the moment they got home.

"There," said Violet, pointing. "Harold Jennings on Mansion Road. That woman who was talking about Becky and her father the first time we met Becky said that's where the Jennings lived."

The Aldens left their house quickly. As they did, Jessie stopped to grab the photograph from the newspaper article that was stuck to the refrigerator. Then the Boxcar Children and Watch raced toward Becky Jennings' house.

When they got near Mansion Road, Watch suddenly barked and pulled ahead. He turned between two huge, open gates set in a high wall, and pulled Jessie with him before she could even see the street number on the wall by the gate.

"I think Watch knows the way," she called.

"He sure does," said Henry, following Jessie. The Aldens rode their bicycles down the long, long driveway and stopped.

The house was indeed a mansion. It was three stories tall and seemed even taller. As they stood there, the door opened. A tall man with a round stomach looked down his nose at the children. It was the butler.

Before the butler could say anything, Jessie said, "We've come to talk to Becky, please."

"One moment, please," said the butler. Soon he returned, looking surprised. "Miss Becky and her father are in the back play area," he said. "I will arrange for someone to take you to them." He raised his hand slightly, and a gardener who had been working in a nearby flowerbed stood up.

"Please take these people and their, er, dog, to Miss Becky," said the butler. "You can go around the side of the house."

The gardener nodded and smiled. She led the children around the side of the house — which was a very long walk — and stopped and pointed. "There she is, over there," said the gardener. "With her father." The gardener left.

But the Aldens didn't go to say hello to Becky right away. They just stopped and stared.

And stared.

Because their boxcar was standing right in the middle of the backyard of the mansion.

Benny spoke first. "Our boxcar!" he shouted and ran toward it, holding Watch's leash. The others hurried after him.

As they got closer, Mr. Jennings stood up. "Look, Becky. Here are your friends coming to visit you," he said.

Becky looked up, too. And she began to scream. She threw her arms around her father's leg. "Go away!" she shouted.

"Becky!" said Mr. Jennings.

"That's our boxcar!" said Benny.

Becky buried her face against her father's leg and began to cry loudly.

But her father ignored her. He bent slightly toward Benny. "What are you talking about, son?" he asked.

"Our boxcar! That's our boxcar!" said Benny.

"See?" said Jessie, stepping up beside Benny and holding out the newspaper clipping.

"Hush, Becky," said Mr. Jennings, stroking his daughter's head with one hand. With the other he held the newspaper clipping and read it.

"Someone stole our boxcar," said Henry. Then the four Aldens told Mr. Jennings what had happened.

Mr. Jennings handed the newspaper clipping back to Jessie. She folded it carefully and put it in her pocket.

"Well, this boxcar is not stolen, I paid for it. However, I did buy it right after yours disappeared. I was out of town so I didn't see the newspaper article," he said. "But that doesn't prove that it is your boxcar."

"Did this boxcar have a table with a blue tablecloth inside? And a cracked pink cup?" asked Violet.

"No!" cried Becky furiously.

"Yes," said Mr. Jennings. "Everything is still in there . . . we haven't started redecorating it yet. But how did you know about those things?"

"Because those were the things in our boxcar," said Violet simply.

Suddenly Watch, who had been very good, barked.

"No!" screamed Becky. "Mean, nasty dog. I don't like that dog!"

Mr. Jennings' eyes widened. He hadn't noticed Watch before. "Why, that's the dog that jumped out of the boxcar when Mr. Winters opened the door for Becky."

"Mr. Winters!" gasped Henry.

"He said it was his dog," Mr. Jennings went on. "He said the dog had just come along for the ride. But the dog barked at him and at Becky and then ran away."

"No," said Benny firmly. "Watch is *our* dog. Mr. Winters was not telling the truth!"

"Mr. Winters," repeated Henry. "A short man who was going bald?"

"Sounds like him. I didn't like him much,

especially after the dog he said was his ran away. Now I see why. And I see that this is your boxcar."

"Mr. Winters tried to buy it from us. He said he wanted it for Senator Teacher's whistle-stop campaign," said Jessie. "He said he worked for Senator Teacher. But when we talked to her, she'd never heard of our boxcar. She told us she had fired Mr. Winters."

"I wonder how he knew that Becky wanted our boxcar?" Henry said.

Mr. Jennings frowned. "I don't know. How strange." Then he stopped frowning. "But we can soon find out. Mr. Winters is supposed to come by this afternoon to get the rest of the payment for the boxcar. I told him I wouldn't pay him all at once until I was sure that we were satisfied with it."

"My playhouse," wailed Becky miserably.

Mr. Jennings bent down and picked his daughter up. "Now, now, Becky. You don't want a stolen playhouse, do you? You couldn't be happy in a playhouse that belongs to someone else. We'll get you a new one."

Becky stared at her father. Then she nodded slowly and put her head against his shoulder.

Smiling and looking a little relieved, Mr. Jennings said, "Why don't you come into the house for milk and cookies until Mr. Winters gets here?"

"And then we will have a big surprise for Mr. Winters," said Jessie. "A very big surprise!"

"Shhh," whispered Henry. "I hear voices." The Aldens had had milk and cookies with Mr. Jennings, Becky, and Martha. Then Becky had gone with Martha to take a nap while the Aldens went back outside. Now they were sitting inside their boxcar behind the almost-closed door.

" . . . not entirely satisfied with this boxcar," they heard Mr. Jennings say.

Mr. Winters' voice said nervously, "Why? It's in very good condition. I fixed it up myself."

"No, he didn't," whispered Benny, outraged. "*We* did!"

"It's not the condition of the boxcar," said Mr. Jennings. "It's what I found inside!" With that he pulled the door of the boxcar open and the Aldens jumped out!

Mr. Winters took a step back. "No!" he cried in amazement. "It can't be you!"

"But it is," said Henry. "You stole our boxcar and we can prove it!"

"I didn't," said Mr. Winters. "Honestly I didn't."

"Then how do you explain having a boxcar that belongs to these children?" asked Mr. Jennings.

"And how do you explain telling Mr. Jennings that our dog Watch was your dog?" demanded Jessie.

Mr. Winters rubbed his hands together nervously. He licked his lips. His eyes darted from side to side. He looked over his shoulder as if he wanted to run away, so Henry grabbed his arm firmly.

"Well?" asked Jessie.

At last Mr. Winters spoke. "Okay, okay, I took your old boxcar. I needed the money, see? I was desperate. I'd just lost my job — "

"We know about that," said Henry. "You were fired for being dishonest!"

Mr. Winters pretended not to notice what Henry had said. He went on, "And I remembered hearing the little girl scream in the street that day that she wanted your boxcar. I happened to be passing by on my way back to the office. I heard her, and that's how I found out about your boxcar. I didn't read about it in the paper."

Mr. Winters sighed. "Even then, I knew that the senator didn't think I was doing a good job. I thought if I could get the boxcar, she'd change her mind. But I didn't get the boxcar and then she fired me anyway."

"That's not *our* fault," said Jessie indignantly.

Again Mr. Winters pretended not to hear. "When I got fired, I remembered that someone else wanted your boxcar. Someone who could afford to pay me a lot of money for it.

So I thought, Why not take it? You didn't need it. And I needed the money."

"You stole our boxcar!" cried Benny.

"I came in the night with a truck that I rented. The dog was inside and began to bark so I slammed the door shut. I couldn't let him out. He would have given me away. I hooked the boxcar to the truck and hauled it away. Then I brought it here, and sold it to Mr. Jennings."

Mr. Winters took a deep breath. "That's all," said Mr. Winters. "That's the whole story."

Mr. Jennings looked at the Aldens. "I will arrange to have your boxcar, and all your belongings that were in it, moved back to your home immediately," he said. "What do you want me to do about Mr. Winters?"

"I think you should call the police," said Henry. "He stole our dog and our boxcar."

"But it wasn't my fault," said Mr. Winters. "It was Senator Teacher's fault for firing me."

"It was not!" said Violet firmly.

Mr. Jennings said, "I'll see to it that the

police take care of Mr. Winters . . . but first, let's see about getting your boxcar safely home!"

"Hooray!" cried Benny. "Hooray! Our boxcar is going home!"

CHAPTER 10

The Parade

"Smile!" said Grandfather Alden. He held up his camera and took a picture of Henry, Jessie, Violet, Benny, Soo Lee, and Watch sitting in the open door of their boxcar. The children wore blue workshirts under their overalls. They were wearing engineer's caps and had red bandannas tied around their necks. Watch had a red bandanna tied around his neck, too.

The boxcar had come safely home. And so, early on the morning of the Founders' Day Parade, Grandfather had hitched it to

his big old truck and pulled it slowly into town. The parade would go right down Main Street where the old railroad track had once run.

Everyone was getting in line to start the parade. People were gathering all along Main Street, shouting and cheering.

Grandfather snapped another picture.

Just then, Violet saw Sam. He was leading Susie down the street. "Look!" she said.

"I can't believe we ever suspected Sam of taking our boxcar," said Jessie in a low voice.

"Me, either," said Henry. "I feel kind of bad that I did."

"Sam! And Susie!" shouted Benny.

"Hello there!" Sam called, leading Susie up to them.

"But where's your wagon?" asked Violet.

"Oh, it's going to be a beautiful new wagon when I finish putting it back together. I wanted it to be a surprise entry in the parade today. Then I found out I had to order new wheels." Sam shook his head, but he was smiling. "But since I'd already polished Susie's harness, I put her in it and we came to the parade anyway."

Another voice spoke. "So this is the famous boxcar — I heard all about what happened! Mr. Jennings is a friend of mine."

"Senator Teacher!" said Henry. "Are you going to be in the parade, too?"

"Hello, Aldens," said the senator. "Yes, I am going to be in the parade." She turned to Grandfather Alden and shook hands with him. "How do you do," said Senator Teacher. "I hope you will vote for me."

"I will," said Benny.

"Then I will, too," said Grandfather Alden, his eyes twinkling.

The senator smiled and turned toward Sam. "I'm Senator Teacher," she said, "and I hope you will vote for me."

"I always have," said Sam.

"Sam's going to be in the parade, too. He has a new wagon that he built, but it's not ready yet. It will be just like his old one that crashed. It's like the caboose on a train," said Jessie. "He can even sleep in it if he wants."

"You can fix things like that?" asked the senator.

"Sure," said Sam.

"I need some help with a truck I'm working on for my whistle-stop campaign," said the senator. "Maybe you could look at the truck after the parade and see if you would be interested in a job fixing that up."

"Why, I'd be glad to," said Sam, looking pleased.

"Great," said the senator. She waved good-bye to the Aldens and went away to shake more hands.

Violet said, "I have an idea. Maybe Susie could pull our boxcar in the parade. If it's okay with you," she said to Sam. To Grandfather she said, "If you don't mind."

"Susie and I would like that," said Sam, stroking Susie's nose. "I could walk alongside her and lead her."

"I think it's a wonderful idea," said Grandfather. "Then I can watch the parade and take lots of pictures."

So Grandfather unhitched the old truck and parked it. Then Sam hitched Susie to the boxcar.

And the parade began.

Grandfather hurried to find a place on the sidewalk to watch the parade. Sam walked beside Susie, holding onto her halter and leading the way.

It was a wonderful parade. It was full of people in historic costumes and beautiful floats. There was even a marching band.

But nothing in the whole parade was as successful as the boxcar with Susie and Sam leading the way. Henry and Jessie and Violet and Benny and Soo Lee waved, and Watch barked and wagged his tail. As they all went by, people cheered loudest of all.

Benny got so excited that he stood up and waved both arms over his head.

"It looks like you are signaling for a train to stop!" said Jessie.

Violet and Soo Loo laughed. Henry grabbed Benny and pulled him back. "You better sit down," said Henry. "Before you fall out and make the whole parade stop!"

Benny sat down again. But he kept waving happily at the crowd. "Oh," said Benny. "I *love* a parade."

GERTRUDE CHANDLER WARNER discovered when she was teaching that many readers who like an exciting story could find no books that were both easy and fun to read. She decided to try to meet this need, and her first book, *The Boxcar Children*, quickly proved she had succeeded.

Miss Warner drew on her own experiences to write each mystery. As a child she spent hours watching trains go by on the tracks opposite her family home. She often dreamed about what it would be like to set up house-keeping in a caboose or freight car — the situation the Alden children find themselves in.

When Miss Warner received requests for more adventures involving Henry, Jessie, Violet, and Benny Alden, she began additional stories. In each, she chose a special setting and introduced unusual or eccentric characters who liked the unpredictable.

While the mystery element is central to each of Miss Warner's books, she never thought of them as strictly juvenile mysteries. She liked to stress the Aldens' independence and resourcefulness and their solid New England devotion to using up and making do. The Aldens go about most of their adventures with as little adult supervision as possible — something else that delights young readers.

Miss Warner lived in Putnam, Connecticut, until her death in 1979. During her lifetime, she received hundreds of letters from girls and boys telling her how much they liked her books.